S0-BNS-380

ArtScroll Youth Series®

Rabbi Nosson Scherman / Rabbi Meir Zlotowitz

General Editors

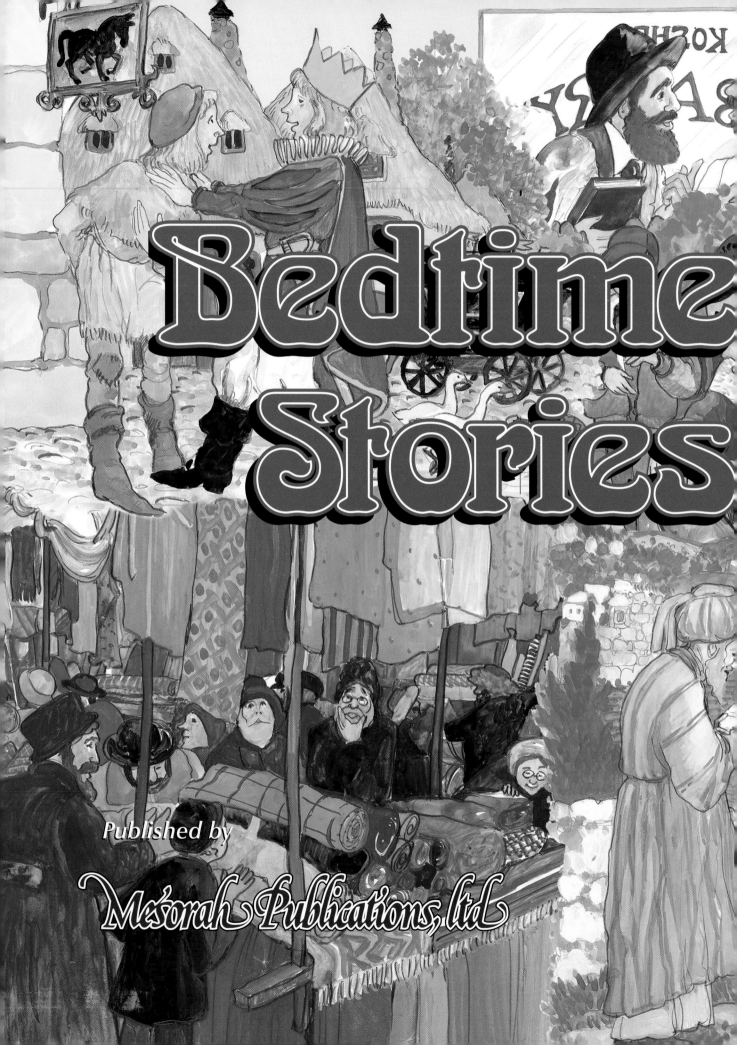

Bedtime Stories

Published by

Mesorah Publications, ltd.

# of Jewish Values

by Shmuel Blitz

Illustrated by Liat Binayamini Ariel

This book is dedicated to my daughter and son-in-law
Daniel and Sarah Aliza Schlesinger

RTSCROLL YOUTH SERIES®

"BEDTIME STORIES OF JEWISH VALUES"

© *Copyright 1998 by* Mesorah Publications, Ltd.
First edition – First impression: March, 1998
           Second impression: July, 1999
           Third impression: September 2002
           Fourth impression: June 2006
           Fifth impression: April 2010

ALL RIGHTS RESERVED

No part of this book may be reproduced **in any form,** *photocopy, electronic media, or otherwise – even FOR PERSONAL, STUDY GROUP, OR CLASSROOM USE – without* **written** *permission from the copyright holder, except by a reviewer who wishes to quote brief passages in connection with a review written for inclusion in magazines or newspapers.*

THE RIGHTS OF THE COPYRIGHT HOLDER WILL BE STRICTLY ENFORCED.

Published by **MESORAH PUBLICATIONS, LTD.**
4401 Second Avenue / Brooklyn, N.Y 11232 / (718) 921-9000 / Fax: (718) 680-1875
www.artscroll.com

Distributed in Israel by SIFRIATI / A. GITLER — BOOKS
6 Hayarkon Street / Bnei Brak 51127

Distributed in Europe by LEHMANNS
Unit E, Viking Business Park, Rolling Mill Road / Jarrow, Tyne and Wear / England NE32 3DP

Distributed in Australia and New Zealand by GOLD'S WORLD OF JUDAICA
3-13 William Street / Balaclava, Melbourne 3183, Victoria, Australia

Distributed in South Africa by KOLLEL BOOKSHOP
Ivy Common, 105 William Road/ Norwood 2192 / Johannesburg, South Africa

Custom bound by Sefercraft, Inc. / 4401 Second Avenue / Brooklyn, N.Y. 11232

ISBN 10: 1-57819-195-5 / ISBN 13: 978-1-57819-195-6

Table of Contents

Do as I Do
An Introduction

BY RABBI NOSSON SCHERMAN

ducators and parents have long known, probably since the beginning of time, that the best way to teach values and mold character is through example. Children are all too quick to note contradictions between our preachments and our practice, and the implied protestation "Do as I say, not as I do" not only falls on deaf ears, it amounts to a crash course in cynicism.

There is another way to teach virtue: through stories. Children love a story. And as they sit with mouth, ears and eyes open, morals — good and bad — seep in through the crevices of their attention. It is an unobtrusive process. Usually its effects will not be noticeable for a long, long time, but effects there will be. Witness the influence of today's entertainment and sports icons on the young people who worship and imitate them. Patterns of dress, vulgarity, loud speech, hair styles, rudeness, loudness and behavior can be traced directly to the media, which bring trendsetters right into the living room and the classroom.

The problem is amplified by the trend toward a "value free" society. We are living in a time when the word virtue has become almost a term of derision, when schools are afraid — indeed, forbidden — to teach values. Whose values? Yours? Mine? Those of a previous generation whose morality has fallen into disrepute?

True, yeshivos and day schools focus on our traditional values, but the home must be an essential part of that equation. To the extent that the common culture permeates the home, there can often be a conflict between school and family, and certainly between the demands of the Torah and the enticements of society. That makes it all the more important that parents — and teachers, too — have the sort of reading materials that can help them in the often unequal struggle against the environment.

Books like this one are a powerful weapon. SHMUEL BLITZ has established himself as a connoisseur who knows how to choose a story and how to tell it. The stories in this book were chosen to make points and to teach subliminally. Whether they are from Rabbinic literature, from the lives of our great people, or parables, whether they are serious or humorous, they teach faith, character, behavior. Beautifully and irresistibly illustrated by LIAT BINYAMINI ARIEL, they will enchant readers and listeners.

Hillel the Elder refuses to be provoked to anger. Rabbi Akiva Eiger would rather be clumsy than let someone else be embarrassed. An older woman learned from youth to understand the importance of visiting the sick. Stories like these leave an impression on malleable minds and — especially if the adults in a child's life are wise enough to set their own positive examples — they can plow deep furrows that will let the seeds of education grow lush and strong.

Readers will applaud this book, as well they should. And we all hope and pray that, with Hashem's help, its fruits will continue to ripen as its readers thrive and grow.

The Velvet Cloth

FAITH

'Leib Mirkes was a holy man who studied Torah day and night. He and his wife owned a fabric store. Every year, he went to the giant fair in Leipzig and bought enough cloth to sell in their store for a whole year.

One year, when R' Leib arrived at the fair, he thought, "What is the rush? The fair will last for a whole month. I will wait until the last day of the fair to buy all the material I need. This way I can spend the whole month learning in the *beis midrash*."

R' Leib walked to the *beis midrash* and began studying.

At the end of the month, R' Leib returned to the fair to buy his material. He went from booth to booth, but everything was sold. All

he could find were three large rolls of expensive red velvet cloth. "I just need to have faith in Hashem," he thought. "He always watches over me." He bought all three rolls and returned home.

R' Leib entered his house and put the three rolls of cloth on the table. "What did you do?" his wife shouted as she saw the expensive fabric. "How will we possibly sell so much red cloth? And now we have nothing else to sell to our regular customers."

"Don't worry," replied R' Leib in a gentle voice. "Just as G-d always helps us sell our regular cloth, He can help us sell this expensive cloth also. We just need to have faith in Him." And R' Leib went off to the *beis midrash* to continue his learning.

During the next two weeks, no matter how much she tried, R' Leib's wife could not sell the red cloth. And each day, R' Leib comforted her by saying, "Don't worry, just have faith in Hashem."

Then one day, two messengers of the king came to their store. "The king needs a large amount of red cloth," said one of the messengers. "We need it to sew new uniforms for all the servants in the palace. Do you have any?"

"Do I have red fabric?" R' Leib's wife was jubilant. She sold him all the red velvet cloth she had. Now she and R' Leib had enough money to last them through the entire next year.

R' Leib realized that it is Hashem Who decides whether a person will be rich or poor. We just need to have faith in Him and do our best. Hashem will take care of the rest.

Ilana and Adina

FRIENDSHIP

lana and Adina were best friends. They played together, studied together and laughed together. They were with each other so much, people thought they were twins. They weren't, but they did have the same birthday.

"This year I am going to buy Adina the most special birthday present," Ilana thought. "I know how much she loves to collect stamps. I will order the newest Israeli stamps for her. To earn enough money, I'll babysit for Mrs. Teicher the first two weeks of the summer."

At that very same moment, Adina was making her own plans. "Ilana is my best friend in the whole world. This year I am going to get her a special present. I know how much she misses her grandparents since they moved to another city. I'll buy her a bus ticket so she can visit them the first two weeks of the summer. To earn enough money, I'll sell my stamp collection."

Both girls worked secretly on their plans to buy each other special birthday presents. Each was so excited about surprising her friend.

Finally, the special day arrived. Adina woke up early, took the bus ticket out of her jewelry box and wrapped it in fancy pink paper. She couldn't wait to give it to her best friend, Ilana.

That same morning Ilana also woke up bright and early. She took the Israeli stamps out of her jewelry box and wrapped them in fancy pink paper. She couldn't wait to give the present to her best friend, Adina.

They both left their houses at the same time. Halfway between their two homes, they met.

"Adina, I have a special present for you," said Ilana. "Here are the newest Israeli stamps. I'll have to babysit every day for the first two weeks of the summer, but I wanted to get you something very special."

Adina stared at the stamps Ilana had just given her. Tears of joy streamed down her cheek. "And here is my present for you. A bus ticket to go visit your grandparents the first two weeks of the summer. I sold my stamp collection to buy it for you."

The two girls hugged each other, knowing they would be friends forever.

True friendship is based on giving to another person, not receiving. To become close with others, we must give a part of ourselves to them. And it is well worth it.

The Precious Stone

INTEGRITY

Reb Yitzchak used to buy and sell rare and precious stones. He owned a valuable blue sapphire. It was worth more than all his other jewels put together.

The king of the land had an idol he worshiped. It had two sapphires for eyes. One morning the king noticed that one of the idol's eyes was gone.

"Who would dare steal the eye of my favorite idol?" thundered the king. "When that man is found, he will be killed. But first, my idol needs a new eye. I want it fast!"

The king's trusted adviser, Salmen, approached. "I know of only one man in the entire kingdom who has such a sapphire. He is a Jew, named Reb Yitzchak."

"Go quickly," ordered the king. "Give him as much money as he wants. Even give him 10 talents of gold for the gem. I want it now!"

Salmen rushed off and boarded a ship to see Reb Yitzchak. A few days later they met. "The king will give you 10 talents of gold for your precious sapphire," offered Salmen. "You surely know that this is much more than it is worth."

"A very generous offer, indeed," Reb Yitzchak replied, "but I cannot sell one of my jewels for idol worship. I cannot accept your offer."

"You *will* accept the offer!" shouted Salmen. "If you don't, I will have you killed and I will take the gem anyway."

Reb Yitzchak saw he had no choice and pretended to agree. The two men boarded the next boat and set sail to bring the jewel to the king.

On the boat, Salmen asked to see the jewel. "It must be so beautiful."

Reb Yitzchak took the jewel out of its pouch and held it up so

Salmen could see it. "Come hold it," said Reb Yitzchak, "but please be careful."

When Salmen tried to take the jewel, Reb Yitzchak pretended his hand was shaking. The jewel was thrown overboard into the water.

"My jewel is lost!" cried Reb Yitzchak. "All that gold is lost!" In truth, this had been his plan. He would not let his jewel be used for idol worship.

Reb Yitzchak and his wife did not have any children. For many years, they had been praying to Hashem for a child they could love and teach. The year after his sapphire was lost, Hashem rewarded Reb Yitzchak with an even more valuable jewel, a son named Shlomo. He grew up to become Rashi, the great teacher of the Jewish people.

Reb Yitzchak was a man of great integrity. Even though it meant losing a large amount of money, he would not allow his jewel to be used for idol worship.

Fresh, Hot Breakfast Rolls

CHARITY

n the 1930s, in the city of Scranton, Pennsylvania, lived a wonderful rabbi named Elchanan Tzvi Guterman. The whole town loved and respected him.

Each morning, the local baker prepared a basket of fresh, hot rolls and left them on the rabbi's doorstep. "He is such a good man," thought the baker. "These hot rolls are just the thing to help him start his day." The rolls were so fresh, one could smell them all the way up the street.

Every morning, Rabbi Guterman opened his door and found the basket of fresh, hot rolls waiting for him and his family. And every day the rabbi called the baker and thanked him for the wonderful present.

One morning, Rabbi Guterman opened his door, and there were no rolls. "I guess the baker was not able to bring the rolls today," he thought.

The next morning, again there were no rolls. "I guess the baker has been very busy and did not have time to send over the rolls," he said to himself. "I will have to check to make sure that the baker is all right. Today, when I buy my Shabbos challos, I will ask how he is feeling."

That afternoon the rabbi arrived at the bakery. "How are you today?" asked Rabbi Guterman. "I hope all is well with you and your family."

"Oh, I'm fine, Rabbi. But how are you?" replied the baker. "I was wondering why you haven't called lately to thank me for the rolls."

A puzzled look appeared on the rabbi's face. "I didn't call because there were no rolls. I thought you were too busy to bring them."

"Too busy for you, Rabbi? Never!" replied the baker. "I left a basket of rolls at your house every day this week, just as I always do."

"Then someone must be taking them before I wake up every morning. We must find that person," said the rabbi.

"Yes, we must find him right away and punish him," added the baker.

"Oh no," said the rabbi. "Not punish him. I said we must *find* him. If he is taking these rolls every day, he must be poor and hungry. We must make sure to get *him* rolls every morning, also. Let's go and try to find him now."

And the two men left together in search of the poor person.

Charity is giving. We might give of our money, time, or even breakfast rolls. If people need charity, we must try to help them in a way that doesn't embarrass them.

The Wager

PATIENCE

ne morning, two men stood in the marketplace talking about Hillel the Sage, the leader of their generation.

"I heard that Hillel is so patient, no one can make him lose his temper," the first man said.

"That's silly," the second man replied. "No one is like that."

"Well, that is what I hear," the first man said. "And I will bet you that you cannot get him angry, no matter how much you try."

"Me, not be able to anger someone? That's a laugh," the second man answered. "I'll bet you a large amount, 400 *zuz,* that I can."

That Friday, not long before Shabbos, the man came outside Hillel's house and yelled, "Where is Hillel? I need to ask him an important question."

Hillel was busy getting ready for Shabbos. He quickly straightened his clothes and went out to the man. "I am here. Come and ask me your question."

The man shouted at Hillel, "Why are the heads of Babylonians shaped like eggs?" The man meant to insult Hillel, who was from Babylonia.

"Hmmm. A very wise question indeed. The heads of Babylonians become egg shaped during birth because their midwives are not well trained." Hillel did not become angry at this silly question.

Frustrated, the man left, only to come back a bit later. He called Hillel again, and Hillel came out. "Hillel, tell me the answer to this question," he shouted. He asked a foolish question about the eyes of people who live in Tadmor.

Based on Talmud *Shabbos* 30b-31a.

The man waited for Hillel to lose his patience. But Hillel replied calmly.

A little later he was back with another silly question, which Hillel patiently answered. Then, even though it was late, Hillel asked if he had any more questions.

Now the man exploded, losing his temper. "If you are Hillel, leader of our generation, I hope there will be no more like you. Because you would not lose your temper, I lost 400 *zuz* in a bet."

"Better you should lose twice that amount of money than that Hillel should lose his temper," the Sage quietly replied.

This incident happened 2000 years ago, yet it is still a lesson for us today. It teaches us how patient each person must be when dealing with others.

Yitzi's Test
PERSEVERANCE

chool can be hard. For Yitzi, school was very hard. One Sunday, Yitzi spent the whole day studying for a test. He saw his friends playing basketball outside his window. "C'mon out, Yitzi," called his friend Avi. "We need you here to play. You're the best shooter we have."

Yitzi wanted very much to go play with his friends. "I'm really sorry," Yitzi answered, "but I have a big *Gemara* test tomorrow, and I need to study."

"So what," yelled Avi. "We all have that same test tomorrow and *we're* playing. Why don't you come out?"

"I need the extra time to study," replied Yitzi.

The next day, the whole class took the *Gemara* test. Yitzi tried very hard. Friday, their rebbi returned the tests, and Yitzi got only a 68. Most of his friends got 80s and 90s.

"Why do I have to work harder than everyone else?" thought Yitzi.

The next Sunday the same thing happened. Yitzi stayed home studying for a *Tanach* test. "Come on out, Yitzi," Avi called. "You're not going to get a good mark anyway. We need one more person to play."

"I'm sorry, but I really want to do well on tomorrow's test," said Yitzi.

So Yitzi stayed home and studied.

The next day, Yitzi again struggled through the test. On Friday, the rebbi returned everyone's test, and Yitzi got a 78.

"See, I told you to play ball instead of studying," teased Avi.

But Yitzi knew that if he hadn't done that extra studying, he wouldn't have passed the test.

The following Sunday the same thing happened again. "Come on out," yelled Avi. "Aren't you going to play ball with us anymore?"

"I'm sorry, but I have a *Chumash* test tomorrow," Yitzi said, "and I really have to study."

The next day, the whole class took the *Chumash* test.

On Friday, before returning the tests, the rebbi announced, "I'd like to congratulate Yitzi. He got a perfect 100 — the highest mark in the class!"

Yitzi sat up in his chair, a big smile slowly appearing on his face.

Yitzi showed perseverance. He did not give up. He kept trying and trying and finally succeeded. Our Sages teach us that we should review what we learn even 400 times if necessary.

Who Is Afraid of Whom?

FEAR OF HEAVEN

n elderly Jew stood on the side of the road. Wrapped in his *tallis,* he swayed back and forth, praying to Hashem.

The silence was broken by the sound of approaching hoofbeats. The Roman general, Pontius, galloped by on his horse. He stopped next to the Jew, waiting to be greeted. Such was the custom in Rome.

The Jew just stood there praying.

Pontius quickly became very angry. "Jew!" he yelled. "Why do you stand there like that and not greet me? You are insulting me."

The Jew did not react. He just stood there, finishing his prayers.

The general was getting angrier and angrier. His face turned red. "You keep on ignoring me?"

Just then the Jew finished praying and turned to General Pontius. "I am very sorry I could not greet you," he said quietly. "I did not mean to be disrespectful. I was in the middle of my morning prayers."

"I don't care what you were doing," Pontius thundered. "I only care that I was insulted."

"I didn't mean to insult you," the Jew said. "Let me explain why I did not answer you."

The Roman general waited impatiently for an explanation.

"Imagine you were talking to the Emperor, and a friend of yours came by. Would you stop and greet your friend?"

"Ignore the Emperor to greet my friend? Of course not," Pontius replied. "The Emperor would have me killed."

"Well then," the Jew continued, "please understand, the Emperor is a king of flesh and blood. He is a man just like you, yet you tremble before him. My G-d is the King of kings, Who lives forever. Should I not tremble when I stand before Him? Should I stop praying to Him to greet you?"

The Roman general understood. He rode away and left the Jew alone.

We must love Hashem, but we must fear Him also. Our Sages teach us that we must fear Hashem at least as much as we fear an ordinary king.

The Special Deal
VISITING THE SICK

or 60 years, Mrs. Leibowitz woke up every morning and went to visit children in the hospital. Everyone called her "the hospital lady." She didn't mind being called that. She just wanted to visit the sick children.

Each morning, Mrs. Leibowitz would see a little girl named Elisheva. "Good morning, Elisheva," she said, with a cheerful smile on her face. "How are you feeling today?"

"Thank you for coming, Mrs. Leibowitz," Elisheva replied. "I look forward to seeing you every day. But I have one question. Why do you spend so much time visiting children in the hospital?"

Mrs. Leibowitz laughed. "I've been visiting children in this hospital every morning now for a long time. It is no trouble at all. It is the nicest part of my day. Our Sages teach us that when we visit a sick person, we take away one tiny bit of their illness. I've seen it. It is true."

"But you do this every day, rain or shine," Elisheva said. "Isn't it

difficult for you? Do you have another reason, too?"

Again, Mrs. Leibowitz chuckled. "Yes, I *do* have another reason. But in all these years I have never told anyone."

"Please tell me," Elisheva whispered. "I really want to know."

"All right, I will tell you," smiled Mrs. Leibowitz. "But it has to be a secret — just between you and me."

A secret! Elisheva loved secrets. She couldn't wait to hear.

"When I was a little girl, just about your age, I was in this hospital, too. The doctors told my mother I was very sick. I prayed very hard to Hashem to make me better. And I made a special deal with Him."

"What kind of special deal?" Elisheva's eyes opened wide in wonder.

"I told Hashem that if He made me better, when I got older, I would visit little children every morning. I did get better, and for 60 years, I've been visiting here every single day. I'm just keeping my promise."

That night Elisheva prayed very hard to get better. And after she finished, she made her own very special deal with Hashem.

When Avraham Avinu was sick, Hashem visited him. If it was important for Hashem to visit the sick, imagine how important it is for us to do the same.

The Stain on the Table
CONSIDERATION FOR OTHERS

The table was beautifully set with white napkins and a crisp white tablecloth. Glasses filled with wine stood next to each dish. A magnificent *Seder* plate crowned the table. It was Pesach, and the guests of Rabbi Akiva Eiger moved to their seats, ready to begin the *Seder*.

All kinds of guests were there; poor people, simple people and wise people. They were all ready to talk about the miracles Hashem did when he took the Jews out of Egypt.

"Come, everyone," Rabbi Akiva Eiger called, "join my family and let us begin the *Seder*."

Everyone gathered around the table for *Kiddush*.

Rabbi Akiva Eiger picked up his silver cup in one hand, ready to begin.

Across the table, one poor old man had difficulty standing. He reached for his own *Kiddush* cup, but instead of grabbing it, knocked it over. The white tablecloth was covered with a giant red stain.

Everyone looked at the old man in shock. He was very embarrassed. He was so ashamed, he could not even open his mouth to say he was sorry.

At that moment, Rabbi Akiva Eiger placed his own cup back on the table. He secretly began shaking the table with his foot. This caused *his* wine to also spill onto the tablecloth. Now the table was stained in two places instead of one.

"Oh my!" said Rabbi Akiva Eiger. "It seems that one of the table's legs is loose and everything is spilling."

Everyone smiled. The old man was not ashamed any more. This

was how R' Akiva Eiger saved the poor old man from being embarrassed in front of all the people.

When we deal with others, think about how they feel. The Sage Hillel teaches us that we should act towards others in the same way that we expect them to act towards us.

A Special Gift
HONOR YOUR PARENTS

"Chaim, did you see the new model airplane my father bought for me?" Yonatan asked.

"Chaim, did you see the new basketball my father got for me?" Elisha asked.

Chaim felt bad. His father was a rebbi in the yeshivah. He didn't earn much money and couldn't buy him special things. "Why can't my father be like the other fathers?" thought Chaim. "I know he's good to me, but I wish I could have some of the things my friends have."

Every night after supper, Chaim's father would say, "Come, Chaim, let's review today's *Gemara.*" That was very nice, but Chaim wanted other things from his father, things his father couldn't afford to give him.

That night, the two sat together studying *Gemara.* But Chaim was not concentrating. He was thinking about what new things his friends would bring to school the next day.

"Chaim, why aren't you paying attention tonight?" his father asked.

"Please tell me what is bothering you."

But Chaim was too embarrassed to tell his father the truth.

The next morning Chaim slowly made his way to school. He was about to walk into the classroom, but stopped when he heard two boys talking.

"Isn't Chaim lucky?" the first boy said. "Every night his father reviews the *Gemara* with him. I wish my father would do that. My father doesn't even get home till I am in bed."

"I know what you mean," added the second. "I wish my father would sit and learn with me at night. I could be the best student in the class."

Chaim couldn't believe what he was hearing. All this time he had been so busy looking at what his friends were receiving, he didn't realize what he had. He finally understood just how special *his* father really was.

The Torah commands us to honor our father and our mother. Our parents want the best for us. We must always be grateful for everything they do.

The Whistle
PROPER PRAYER

ri was a shepherd. This year he would be 13 and become *bar mitzvah*. He was very excited. But because Ari's family was so poor, he spent his whole day watching sheep. He had never gone to yeshivah, had never been in *shul,* and did not know how to read.

He tenderly cared for the sheep. He had a name for each one of them. "Come to me, my little friends," he would say. When he whistled, all the sheep came running to him. His whistle could be heard all over the meadow.

"But what shall I do about my *bar mitzvah*?" he thought. "I do not know how to pray." He decided to go to *shul* and see what people do there.

On Shabbos morning he dressed in his best clothes and left his house early for the long walk to *shul.* He saw all the men wearing *taleisim.* People swayed back and forth as they prayed. He watched and watched. He wanted to pray like them, but he didn't know how.

Ari was lost. He didn't know what to do.

He took a small *siddur* from a shelf and held it in his hand. He kissed it and clutched it close to his chest.

"What shall I do?" he thought. "I don't know how to pray like these other people."

Suddenly, he pursed his lips together and let out a loud whistle. The whistle came from his heart and soul. He whistled loud and clear. He whistled and whistled.

"Shhh," a man scolded him. "What are you doing? This is a *shul*!"

The rabbi raised his hand. "My dear people," the rabbi said, "you don't understand. Let this boy whistle. That is his prayer. His prayer is pure and simple, rising directly to Hashem. If only *we* could pray with such purity and match the holiness of his prayer!"

Hashem wants us close to Him. Prayer helps bring us closer to Hashem. Each person must pray with all his heart. Sometimes, even a simple whistle can be important to Hashem, if it is sincere.

Orit's Birthday
JUDGING OTHERS FAVORABLY

rit woke up early in the morning. It was her birthday, and she had been looking forward to this day for weeks. She dressed quickly, ate breakfast and ran off to school.

"Tamar," said Orit, "do you know that today is my birthday?"

"Oh, is it? That's nice," replied Tamar. "Have a happy birthday."

Orit was surprised that Tamar wasn't more excited. So she went over to her best friend, Shaindel. "Shaindel, did you know that today is my birthday?"

"Mmmm. Happy birthday," replied Shaindel as she walked away talking to another girl.

Orit felt very bad. "Why doesn't anybody care that today is my birthday?"

She invited some girls to come to her house that afternoon to play. But no one would come. Her friends were too busy with other things.

"This is the worst birthday I've ever had. I have no friends."

The school bell finally rang. All the children rushed out of school. "This was a very bad day," Orit thought. "Everyone is ignoring me." She was so sad.

Orit walked home very slowly. "I have the worst friends in the whole world. I'll never talk to any of them ever again. Nobody likes me, and I don't like them."

When she came home, Orit opened the front door. Before she even put down her schoolbooks, she heard a loud yell, "SURPRISE." All her friends jumped out from behind the curtains, from behind the sofa and from behind the chairs, singing, "Happy Birthday."

Orit's eyes opened wide in surprise. She was so happy. She had the best friends any girl could ever want.

We should always judge other people favorably. Sometimes it seems that they are acting wrongly. But we may not know all the facts. We should assume that they are doing the right thing.

The Shepherd

COMPASSION

Before he led the Jewish people, Moshe Rabbeinu was a shepherd. He watched his sheep carefully and made sure nothing bad happened to them. In the winter he protected them from the cold, and in the summer from the hot sun.

Each day, he divided the sheep into three groups. First, he let the babies graze. Their teeth were the smallest and, therefore, they ate the softest grass. After they finished, he allowed the middle-sized sheep to eat. And after they finished, the oldest sheep grazed. Their teeth were the strongest, and they ate the toughest grass left over by the others.

Based on *Shemos Rabbah* 2:2.

Once, one little sheep ran away. Moshe searched all over the mountains and the desert. Finally, he found it drinking from a pond. "You must be so thirsty," Moshe said to the sheep. "No wonder you ran away. Come here and I will carry you back to your flock."

Hashem saw how kind Moshe was to the animals. "Moshe will be the perfect one to lead My children, the Jewish people, out of Egypt," Hashem said.

Hashem appeared to Moshe in a burning bush. The bush was on fire, but it did not burn up.

"Moshe, Moshe, I am the G-d of your fathers, Avraham, Yitzchak and Yaakov," Hashem said to him.

Moshe was afraid and hid his face.

"Now I am making you My messenger," G-d continued. "You will take My children out of Egypt. Their cries of pain have reached Me in Heaven. I am sending you to bring them to freedom."

Moshe listened to Hashem and brought the Jews out of Egypt. Then, he led them to Mount Sinai where Hashem gave them the Ten Commandments.

Hashem saw how compassionate Moshe was with animals. All of us should be kind. If we are expected to be this kind to animals, imagine how kind we must be to other people!

Trading Places
CONTENTMENT

In a faraway land there lived a young prince named Randolph who ruled over many people. But he was not happy. "It is so lonely being the prince," he thought. "I wish I had friends to play with."

In a small village nearby lived a poor boy named Kapi. "There is nothing in our house to eat," he thought. "And there is no wood left in the stove. I wish I were the prince and could just play and relax in the palace every day."

One day Prince Randolph went for a walk. Passing through a village, he saw Kapi. "This is amazing. You look just like me," said the prince to the boy.

"And you look just like me," Kapi replied.

"I have a wonderful idea," suggested the prince. "Why don't we trade places for one week? You can go live in the palace, and I will stay here in your village."

Kapi was thrilled with the idea. He ran off to the palace, looking forward to beginning his week as a prince.

The first day, Kapi had a grand time. He ate the most delicious foods and slept in the royal bed with fluffy pillows and warm feather quilts. But after three days, he became bored. "There is no one here to play with. I am so lonely. I wish some of my friends were here."

In the village, Prince Randolph was having a great time playing with all of Kapi's friends. But at night there was little to eat. In the house it was so cold, it was hard to sleep. After three days, he missed the royal palace.

The week passed and each boy rushed to see how the other was doing.

"Kapi, it was nice living in your house," said the prince. "But I am glad to return to the royal palace."

"The palace is a fine place to live," Kapi replied, "but I can't wait to see all my friends. I, too, am glad the week is over."

The two boys returned to their homes, and each one was thankful for what he had.

Our Sages teach us, "Who is rich? The person who is happy with what he has." Hashem wants us to be satisfied and content with what He gave us and not want what other people have.

The Special Penny
HONESTY

aftali celebrated his 9th birthday. He received many nice gifts. But the present from Uncle Moishe excited him most — $50. Naftali knew just what he wanted to do with that money.

Naftali had the best coin collection around. Not only did he have many valuable coins, but he even had rare coins from other countries. He had coins from Israel, Africa and even Japan.

But his friend Yitzchak owned the one coin he wanted most. It was an old 1955 S penny, minted in San Francisco. It was one of the rarest pennies ever made. He was especially excited because he heard that Yitzchak was willing to sell it. The next morning during *davening,* Naftali rushed over to Yitzchak.

"Yitzchak, I hear you are willing to sell your 1955 S penny," Naftali began. "I want to buy it so much. Yesterday was my birthday, and I have enough money," he exclaimed. "I'll tell you what, I'll give you $35 for it."

Yitzchak was in the middle of *davening,* so he didn't respond.

Naftali thought Yitzchak didn't say anything because he wanted more money. "You're right," Naftali said, "that coin is worth more than $35. I'll give you *$50.* Just please sell me the penny."

Yitzchak was still *davening,* so again he didn't respond.

"You *must* sell me that coin. I want it more than anything!" Naftali insisted. He offered to pay $75 for the rare 1955 S penny, even though he didn't know how he would get that much money.

Just then Yitzchak finished *davening.* "Naftali," he said, "when you offered me $35 for the coin, I felt it was a fair price and decided to sell it to you for that amount. I didn't answer because I was in the middle of *davening*. You don't have to pay me more than that. The penny is yours."

Naftali stared at Yitzchak in amazement, so impressed with his honesty.

A person must be honest in all his dealings. Even if he can fool someone else, he must always tell the truth.

The Right Match

LOVE OF TORAH

It was time for Rabbi Eizl Charif's daughter to get married. He wanted to find just the right husband for her.

"I will search in all the great yeshivos to find the best young man for her," he decided. "I know how to pick the right one."

R' Eizl visited the most famous yeshivah in Poland. All the young men ran to greet him. They were so excited to meet one of the great leaders of the generation.

R' Eizl said to the students, "I will now ask a very hard question on the *Gemara*. Whoever knows the answer will be considered as a match to marry my daughter."

"Marry the daughter of R' Eizl?" they murmured to each other. "What an honor that would be!"

One by one, the students tried to answer his question. No one knew the right answer. The question was too difficult for them.

R' Eizl went to the next yeshivah. "Whoever can answer this question on the *Gemara* will have a chance to marry my daughter," he said. Again, every student tried to find an answer, but no one could. The question was too difficult for them.

R' Eizl visited a third yeshivah. Again he asked his question, but no one could think of the right answer. The question was too difficult for them.

R' Eizl began walking to his carriage. Suddenly, one young man came running after him. "R' Eizl, R' Eizl, please wait. I must talk to you. You asked such a beautiful question. I can't solve the problem, but I beg you to tell me the answer. I need to understand the *Gemara*. I won't be able to sleep until I know the answer. Please don't leave without telling me."

R' Eizl smiled at the young man. "I see that you really have a love of Torah," he explained. "You didn't just give up. You really wanted to know the answer. You are the kind of person who should marry my daughter. Because of your special love of Torah, you will one day become a great *talmid chacham* and a leader of the Jewish people."

The Torah is a special present given to us by Hashem. We must love and cherish it and devote our life to learning it.

You Get What You Pay For

WELCOMING GUESTS

hree visitors arrived in town one Friday. They were told they could stay at Reuven Katz's house for Shabbos. Reuven loved having guests join him.

He welcomed them into his home. "Here is the room you will stay in," Reuven told them. "Please make yourselves comfortable. And one more thing. I charge each person who stays in my house for Shabbos $25. But for that price, you can eat and drink as much as you want."

The guests were a bit surprised. After Reuven had left, the first man complained, "I thought we would be staying here as guests. No

one told us we would have to pay."

"Well, since we have to pay," the second man said, "let's make the best of it and eat and drink as much as we like."

"And I'll be sure to get my money's worth," chimed in the third man.

That Shabbos all three guests had a wonderful time. They ate their fill, talked, sang and discussed Torah topics.

After Shabbos, the three men came to pay Reuven for their stay. "This was a very nice Shabbos. It was well worth the $25 you charged," said the first man.

"You certainly have earned your fee," added the second man.

"And I surely got my money's worth," chuckled the third.

"Oh no," Reuven replied. "I won't take your money. You were my guests. I only told you I would charge you so you would enjoy yourself and eat as much as you wanted. I wanted you to feel like you were in your own home. The next time you are in town please join me for another full Shabbos meal. And, of course, it will again be my treat."

We must make guests feel at home. Hashem was joyous when our forefather, Avraham, welcomed his guests in a full and open manner.

David and Goliath
COURAGE

Goliath was a giant. He stood about 12 feet tall. He led the Philistines in their war against the Jewish people.

"Choose someone to come fight against me," he thundered. "Isn't there a Jew who is brave enough?" Goliath was wearing his metal helmet and armor, and holding a huge spear. The Jews were terrified.

"Who will go fight him?" King Saul asked. "I shall greatly reward

anyone who will beat him."

But no one had the courage to stand up against Goliath.

Almost no one.

David was a shepherd and his brothers were in King Saul's army. One morning, his father sent David to bring food to his brothers.

When David arrived at the battlefield, he saw everyone standing there, frightened. "We cannot let Goliath insult Hashem. Isn't there anyone who will stand up against him?" David asked.

David approached King Saul and said, "I will fight this man. And I

Based on *I Samuel* Chap. 17.

will win. Hashem will be with me."

"But you are just a lad, and Goliath has been a warrior all his life," replied the king.

"I am a shepherd," answered David, "and every day, with Hashem's help, I protect my sheep from lions and bears. Hashem is with me. He will help me again today."

David put his slingshot in his pocket, picked up a few smooth rocks, and approached Goliath.

Goliath laughed. "This is who you send me? I will finish him quickly."

David stared into the giant's eyes. "You may have a sword, but I come to you in the name of Hashem. And

with Hashem's help I will kill you today."

Goliath charged toward the boy. David grabbed his slingshot, loaded a stone onto it, and shot it at the giant. The rock hit Goliath on his forehead, right between his eyes. There was a look of shock on Goliath's face as he fell to the ground, dead.

With Hashem's help, little David defeated the giant.

A person must always show courage. Sometimes we need to fight big giants and sometimes little giants. But there is never anything to fear when we do Hashem's will. We know He will always help us.

And the Angels Smiled

FORGIVENESS

"**O**uch! You stepped right on my toe," hollered Nachum. "Why can't you be more careful?"

"I'm sorry," Yoni apologized, "it was an accident."

"You may say you're sorry, but my foot still hurts," said Nachum.

Up in heaven the angels must have been crying.

"Mom, you said my white shirt would be ironed today," complained Nachum. "Now I don't have a clean shirt to wear to school."

"I'm sorry, Nachum," his mother replied. "But today was your little sister's birthday party. I didn't have time for anything else."

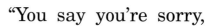

"You say you're sorry, but I still don't have a white shirt for school," yelled Nachum.

Up in heaven the angels must have been crying.

"I'm sorry, class," Mrs. Fleischman apologized, "but because of the bus strike, we can't go to the zoo today."

"We can't go?" shouted Nachum. "We waited all month to go to the zoo. You may say you're sorry, but we're the ones who are missing the big trip."

Up in heaven the angels must have been crying.

Rosh Hashanah arrived and Nachum *davened* in *shul*. He prayed very hard, just like everyone else. That night Nachum had a dream. Up in heaven, he saw his Book of Deeds being reviewed.

"Nachum prayed very hard for forgiveness this year," a deep voice announced. "But when I look at his deeds, I see he didn't forgive anyone else. How can he be forgiven for his sins, if he doesn't forgive anyone else?"

In Nachum's dream, the angels in heaven were crying.

During recess the next day, the boys were playing with Nachum's ball. Aryeh hit the ball so hard, it flew into the bushes. No one could find it. Aryeh said to Nachum, "I'm very sorry. I really tried to find your ball, but it's lost."

"Oh, don't worry about it," Nachum answered with a smile. "It was an accident that could happen to anyone. I accept your apology."

And up in heaven the angels must have smiled.

Everyone makes mistakes. If we repent properly, Hashem is always ready to forgive us. But that is only if we are ready to forgive others, too.

The King's Cure
PROPER SPEECH

The king was very sick. His doctors gathered around him and decided, "Only one thing can save the king. He must drink the milk of a lioness."

One faithful servant offered to get the milk for the king. He had an idea how to accomplish this difficult job. He took a large sack of meat to the forest and found a lioness with her baby cubs. Each day he gave the lioness some meat. Each day he got a little closer, until the lioness trusted him. Soon, he got close enough to get milk from her.

That night the servant had a strange dream. His limbs were arguing about who deserved the most credit for getting the milk.

"I was most important," said his legs. "I brought us closer to the lioness every day."

"No, I was most important," boasted the heart. "It was my courage that allowed us to succeed."

The little tongue spoke up. "No, my friends, it was me. I told the king that we would get the milk."

All the limbs laughed at the tongue. "You are so tiny and weak!"

But the tongue said, "Tiny and weak? I'll show all of you what a tongue can do. I'll prove how powerful I am!"

The next morning the servant brought the lioness's milk to the king. "Here, Your Majesty. I have brought you the milk from a dog."

"Milk from a dog?" the king shouted. "I need milk from a lioness! Throw this man into prison and have him killed tomorrow."

That night the servant had another dream. "Now you see that I am the most powerful?" asked the tongue.

"Tomorrow morning I will show you how this tiny and weak tongue can save you!"

In the morning, the prison guards woke the servant. "Please, I must talk to the king immediately," the man begged.

They brought him to the king. "Forgive me, Your Majesty, but I made a terrible mistake yesterday. I said the milk was from a dog. Believe me, the milk I brought you is from a lioness. Drink it, and you will see."

The king drank the milk and was cured immediately. The servant was rewarded with much gold and honor for saving the king's life.

The tongue is very powerful. It can hold the power of life and death. We must be careful of everything we say and think before we speak.

Glossary

bar Mitzvah:	13th year, the age a boy reaches manhood
beis midrash:	study hall
Chumash:	the Five Books of Moses
davening:	praying
Gemara:	Talmud
Kiddush:	blessing said over wine at Sabbath and Festival meals
Seder:	The festive meal eaten on the first two nights of Passover (in Israel only the first night)
shul:	synagogue
tallis (talleisim):	prayer shawl(s)
talmid chacham:	learned person
Tanach:	Bible
zuz:	coin